Ella's Journey

A Whig Fairy Tale

Ella's Journey

A Whig Fairy Tale

S. R. Harris

Pacific Book Publishing
Washington

Also by S. R. Harris

The Ballad of Fox

Light on the Land

Hackamore Lore

Pacific Book Publishing LLC

8911 Vernon RD #125, Lake Stevens, Washington

www.Pacific-Books.com

ISBN: 9781737329114

Printed in the United States of America

CONTENTS

Beloved Caiti

As we came home from Faithe's funeral,

you asked for a story…

I

Treasure

Sweet music swelled to fill the ballroom. The crown prince slept through the celebration of his sixth birthday, but the music played on. Glow of a thousand beeswax candles sparkled in the crystal facets of chandeliers. Dancers swirled and swayed over the polished marble floor. Light glanced on jeweled pins and silken brocade, on the gold-flecked gowns of gracious women, and the uniforms of dignified men.

Her eyes shone brighter than the crystal, her face and form fairer than any hoarded gem. In his arms Lord Davis held treasure more precious than the prince's throne, and the young lovers were glad. Music overflowed the ballroom and

seeped through the palace; it trickled into the kitchen where servants prepared refreshments for their betters; it drifted over the homes of weary craftsmen, and calculating merchants; it flowed on a cold night wind, past penniless people who tended small fires, or huddled, longing for morning; it faded at last in snowy forests where wolves crouched, waiting.

~

Hannah Grint looked from a kitchen window down into the manor house garden. She heard the quiet laughter of the Lord and Lady where they sat under an arbor, thymian blooming at their feet, a tiny, cooing bundle in their arms. She carried out a tray and set it near the family. Her strong, brown hands tenderly poured chamomile tea as she smiled on the baby who would someday be Lady Davis, "Sweetest bloom in a summer of flowers…"

The young mother smiled, her eyes a flash of blue as her frail, white hand took the mug. "Thank you, Hannah."

Mrs. Grint's fingers brushed the baby's wisp of golden hair. "I rocked her daddy on this very bench when he was a *junge*,[1] he played here with my little *schätze*[2] – long under sod in the churchyard now."

"Peace be upon them," murmured Lady and Lord Davis together. He stood, kissed his wife and daughter, and carried his hoe back to the fields.

"His brother threw the inheritance on the ground, and my Lord will grow it back out of the ground," Hannah observed.

---

[1]*Junge* – 'Youngster' *German.*
[2] *Schätze* – 'Treasures', as in 'My beloved children' *German.*

3

"I am glad he has your Grint," Lady Davis smiled, "the demesne[3] is too much work for a man alone." A breeze blew through the garden, cool from the mountains. She shivered.

"You rest here my Lady." Hannah brushed the cushion, shook out a folded blanket, and spread it over her mistress. She took the baby as Lady Davis lay back. "I will rock little Sunshine, you rest in the sunshine." She patted the baby and purred, looking out through the garden gate where her husband hoed weeds beside the Lord of the Manor. Lady Davis breathed quietly behind them. "Hmm Mausi," Hannah whispered, "a lesser man never could, never could, but your Daddy may. He is a Rider, like your grandfather. With my Grint and the help of the holy Isidore[4], he may undo all the wrong your uncle did.

~

"… lux … sum … mundi." Ella's tiny mouth echoed her mother as her eyes followed her finger on the page. The little girl wiggled and Lady Davis set her down to dance in the garden, golden hair flying. Her mother and Hannah laughed, Rufus leaped and barked, and the squealing child chased him out of the garden.

---

[3] Demesne lands were farmed for the support of the manor rather than being sub-enfeoffed or leased out for cash.

[4] Isidore is the patron saint of farmers and agriculture.

4

Hannah set aside her lavender braid and gathered up the Alemannic Froschauer Bible,[5] and the poems Antiquités de Rome.[6] Lady Davis stood as Ella raced back into the yard. She lifted the Latin volume, and lugged it through the kitchen and dining hall, into the Long Gallery where a faded medieval tapestry hung between gilt-framed portraits. Lady Davis rippled the heavy cloth and the unicorn in his garden seemed to dance. The three women slipped behind the tapestry, Lady Davis opened a door there, and stepped up into a hidden chamber.

Light filtered from windows high above. A dictionary[7] sat enthroned upon a marble plinth. Four tall shelves stood grand and grim as ancient trees in a fairy forest. The women set the volumes on their shelves. Ella looked up at the slanting beams of light and dust dancing, like the words in all the books, waiting for her to grow tall enough to reach them.

~

---

[5] The Alemannic Froschauer Bible is an illustrated masterpiece in proto-Swiss-German, based on the translations of Zwingli and Luther. It was first printed in its entirety in 1530.

[6] "Antiquités de Rome" is a collection of sonnets in literary French by Joachim du Bellay, published in 1558.

[7] Dictionary "Die teütsch Spraach" was published in 1561 by the Swiss pastor, bookbinder and lexicographer Josua Maaler. This scholarly work is written in Alemannic and Latin.

Hand in hand they walked together across the demesne fields to the creek. Six-year-old Ella splashed while her parents sat in the summertime shade of a spreading ash tree.

Her father called, "Ella, come." She released a minnow from her cupped hands, and turned to see Lord Davis gently lifting his wife in his arms.

"Is mother sleeping?" she asked.

"Yes. Come along now," She had to run to keep up with him.

The manor house became strange then. Doctors and apothecaries came and went. Mrs. Grint seemed never to sleep. When little Ella awoke in the morning, she found the kitchen already bright with fire. When she awoke in the night, Mrs. Grint was in the solar, rocking on the bench her husband had made. Then Ella would sit beside her, and the old woman would wrap the end of her shawl around the child until she fell asleep to Hannah's droning sing-song, and the click of her rosary.

Mrs. Grint was gone one afternoon when Ella peeked into her mother's room. Sunshine flowed in the window, lighting a halo of gold and copper hair around Lady Davis' peaked face. Her mother beckoned. Ella set her handful of flowers on the foot of the bed and snuggled close.

"Ella."

"Yes mother?"

"Ella will you always follow the Lord Jesus with all your heart?"

"Yes mother, I will always."

Lady Davis smiled. "And you will always be a brave girl, and work hard, and help daddy?"

"Yes mother."

"That's my good girl," her mother sighed. Her hand rested cool on Ella's brow. The child felt how thin her mother's body had become. "I am proud of you Ella. I love you…"

"I love you too mother." Ella felt strange inside, "Mother, I am going to play with Hound Rufus by the stable. Shall I ask father to come to you?"

"…Yes." So quiet.

Rain came that afternoon. Ella played in the stable with the dog, and then set her dollies to keeping house together. When it grew late, she made a bit of porridge for supper and put herself to bed. The kitchen was cold when Ella awoke in the morning. She heard hammering in the stable, and followed the sound to where her father and Grint worked together. She stood and watched them. No one spoke. They had made a box. Long. Of pale wood.

Lord Davis went out and returned a few minutes later, carrying his wife in his arms. Grint spread a blanket over the box. Lord Davis lay the woman inside with her pale hands clasped on her breast. Gently he folded the blanket over her, leaving her face exposed. Grint hitched up the horse, and he and Lord Davis set the coffin and lid into the wagon.

The tiny chapel stood silent and empty when Lord Davis and Grint began to dig. Lilies of purity grew in profusion around the churchyard. Ella gathered them as the men dug. They set the coffin beside the open grave.

Ella lay a bouquet on her mother's hands and leaned down to kiss her cold brow.

Lord Davis knelt there for a time.

He stood.

They nailed shut the coffin, lowered it into the grave, and began shoveling dark earth and bits of bone back into the hole.

II

Together

Hound Rufus greeted Ella with a tail-thump. She rubbed his ears, and then brushed the smooring ashes aside and set the morning fire.

When Lord Davis came in from the stable, tea was steeping and the porridge ready. Together they knelt by the hearth, then sat up to the table.

"Daddy…"

"Ella?"

"Daddy, what is the work today?"

"Can you guess?" He smiled.

"Harrowing?"

Head shake.

"Weeding?"

He chuckled, "There is always weeding! But today we will let them grow!"

She guessed again, "Setting in pumpkins?" She pointed to a tray where tiny green leaves poked up from the mulch.

"Today we must drown worms!" Lord Davis laughed. Ella jumped from the table with a squeal and clapped her hands. "I am proud of you Ella, you keep our house, tend our garden, and help me in the fields. You hardly have time to be a lady – and there is much a lady must learn! Someday, I will teach you to dance, but today we will practice fishing!"

As they walked, hand-in-hand across the field, Lord Davis looked at his daughter and heir. Her cheeks were brown, her limbs strong, her hair streaked with pale gold from days spent working in the spring sunshine. He felt her hand, rough, in his. She sensed his attention and smiled up, her eyes a flash of blue – like her mother's. Five years. Long years. Fast years.

"Ella, are you lonely ever?"

She thought for a moment. "No. I miss mother, but when I open the Bible, I hear her voice reading to me. I think of her when the lavender blooms. I like to help Mrs. Grint in her garden, and to dig with you in ours. Sometimes I play with the thatcher's children. And I have Rufus!" She leaned out to stroke the dog's back as he loped past.

Lord Davis smiled at his daughter.

That night, after their cena of fish and tea, he sat alone by the fire, thinking with the leaping flames, with the settling coals. After morning chores, he brushed and washed his saddlehorse, bathed himself, dressed for court, and rode away toward the town and castle.

The sun marked hours as Ella waited for her father's return. She left the kitchen door open as darkness fell, and listened for the sound of his horse. At last, as the moon silvered the newly planted pumpkins, she heard hooves clipping through the night.

Her father came home with a smile. Ella set him up to the table and noticed that he sat very straight, and ate his simple meal with dignity. She waited politely until he pushed back his plate and smiled. Ella slid a cup of mint clarea[8] toward him, and smiled her question.

"Dear Daughter, next week I will have a surprise for you! I believe it will make you very, very glad!"

"Daddy I am glad! But what is the surprise?" He stood, kissed her brow, lit his candle from the table lamp, and went whistling to his chambers.

The next day, and the one after, Mrs. Grint and Ella scrubbed and cleaned. Most of the manor house had been closed since the days of Lord Davis' predecessor, for there had been little money to pay servants, and few guests visited the Davis Lands. Ella and her father had kept the solar, and two rooms in the upper hall, but the kitchen was

---

[8] Clarea was popular among all medieval and renaissance classes. The beverage was made of honey and spices, boiled and cooled, and served with a meal. Recipes for this traditional, non-alcoholic drink can be found in the *Llibre del Coch/Libro de Cocina 1520*.

the only room they warmed. Father and daughter often slept there on cold nights. But now all the rooms of the upper hall were turned out for cleaning. The solar was swept and scrubbed, and every candle reflector polished until it shone with medieval splendor. Silverware Ella had never seen was brought out and polished bright. Washed linens fluttered, drying on a line outside. The tall carven door of the Long Gallery was scraped, oiled, and rubbed. It glowed proudly, willing to welcome any visitor to Davis Hall.

Mrs. Grint, who knew about such things, burnt fragrant herbs in the solar. The house seemed strange and lovely to Ella; she wondered if this was how the manor house had looked in the days when ten knights and seventy crossbows had followed her great great Grandfather to war. She imagined that the portraits of her ancestors in the Long Gallery looked pleased.

At last! The cleaning was done. Ella obeyed Mrs. Grint as she adorned the small dining hall and prepared food fit for the gleaming silver and crystal settings. Mrs. Grint grumbled, "To think that this was never done for the *real* Lady Davis!" Ella looked a question, but the old woman shook her head, and went on with the preparations.

Ella wandered outside. Lavender fragrance filled the garden. She remembered her mother's joy as she gathered an armload.

Ella heard the clatter of wheels and looked up the road. Yes! It was their horse and carriage, but it seemed to be full of people... She shaded her eyes. Lord Davis was driving... and beside him sat a woman! Ella ran and stood beside the gallery door.

The carriage stopped and Lord Davis smiled down at his daughter. She stared up at him, her arms still full of lavender. "Ella! This is your new mother! She is going to help you learn to be a lady." He turned to the woman at his side, very tall, with a pale, narrow face and dark eyes. "Heloise, this is my daughter Ella Andrea Esmée Sophia

Davis.[9]" Ella stared. Her father climbed down, and reached a hand up to the tall woman, who kept her gaze fixed upon Ella. She stepped down and stood at Lord Davis' side. She gave a stiff half-curtsey and said, "Lady Davis."

Ella heard her own voice say, "Welcome to Davis Manor."

Then the tall woman swept past her and up the steps of the house. Ella heard a thin ringing as of glass stressed to the breaking point. Her lips and hands felt cold and prickly. The sky and land blurred as she turned back to the carriage. Dimly she saw two girls not much older than herself sitting in gowns well-made, worn, and carefully mended. Ella saw their jewelry of polished brass and red glass. She saw their pale, pretty faces hard-lined, and their dark eyes staring at her. From a distance she heard her

---

[9] Ella – from the Welsh: She delights in life, the Beautiful One.
Andrea – from the German: Defender of Mankind, referring to St Andrew.
Esmée – from the French: Loved, or Beloved.
Sophia – from the Greek, but popular in many lands: Wise One.
Davis – from the Welsh: Descendent of David.

father's voice. "And this is s…asf…fjs… d..w.s…a…." his words lost meaning. Dimly, she saw the girls step down, curtsey, and disappear from her view. Something cold touched her hand. Then birds were singing again, light shone on the mossy walls and polished door of her ancestral home. Rufus' tail thumped her leg and he thrust his nose into her hand again. She stroked him and said, "Hound. Hound…"

She saw her father in the doorway. "Ella," he said, coming down the steps and taking her hand. He put his other hand on the bridle and the horse walked with them. "I have surprised you Ella, forgive me. I did not know if Heloise would marry me, I did not know until today. I had hoped so, as much for you as for me."

"But Daddy, aren't you happy with me?" Ella whispered.

In the stable's sweet shade he unhitched the horse and handed Ella a curry. She began on the horse as he wiped the harness and hung it up. "My dear, what are you doing?" His voice was tender.

"I curry the horse like you taught me…"

"Yes. I taught you this. When you are older I will teach you to handle a sword, yes and pike, and musket too – peace is ever tenuous. We will work together with Grint. We will pay our debts and save the manor... But Ella, what will *you* do?"

She was puzzled, "The 'Next Right Thing,' like you and mother taught me."

He looked out over the fields for a long moment. Ella curried. At last he said, "Ella, as a Mesne Lord[10] I must go to court. You, too, will spend time there. You must learn how to deport yourself with others. Life is not always simple. You need a mother to help you learn. When I was in the army, we were twice transported on ships. I remember the care and skill with which those sways were manned, and the horses tied to the hurdles… It is different than rowing a boat!"

---

[10] A Mesne Lord held lands from a feudal superior, and had land-holding vassals under him. This noble had responsibilities in the court and army of his lord. He was attended there by a retinue of his own family and vassals.

"Daddy I do not understand what this has to do with… with *Her.*"

The horse was cool. Lord Davis let him drink, forked hay into the manger, and shut the stall. The horse trotted into his paddock and lay down to roll. "Ella, there is much to being a woman, so much to being a lady, that I cannot teach you. Heloise and her daughters will help you learn to be a lady, and our home will be good for them – she was a widow, and lonely. They were guests of the prince for a long time; the palace is not a good place for her daughters to be guests without wealth or father. Together we can rebuild the Davis house and fortune. Worthy young suitors will come here. I will ward her daughters until they are wed. We will be a family together. Someday, you will be the Lady Davis. Will you be brave Ella? Will you help me? I know it will not be easy."

Ella stepped close and he wrapped his arms around her. She pressed her ear to his chest, and heard his heart beating strongly… "Yes, Daddy."

III

Alone

Rain slashed the windows and sloshed in the gutters. Ella sat close to her candle, feeling its tiny heat as she poured over the book in her lap. The kitchen would be warmer. But *they* were there. Soon she would go down and serve supper. Soon. But not yet.

The words blurred before her and she rested her head on the page, remembering... Grint shouting. The harrow upturned. Her father, dirty, pale. Blood on his face. She was gasping, reaching, trying to help him, to heal him.

His words, quiet words, "Love... love... love..." Grint dug alone. Dark the hole. Alone he lowered the body. Ella stood numbly beside him in the dark churchyard. She lay on the cold mound... for an hour? A day? Three days? The candle beside her guttered. Ella pinched it out and stared into the sudden darkness. Four years ago? It was four years. Four years.

Years when money-lenders had come to the manor, and left with mortgages against her father's fields and mill. The portraits of her ancestors had rolled away in carts. The buyers left behind small sacks of silver which were soon spent. One dreadful day she found her step-mother wheedling with a rag merchant. "No!" he snapped, waving a hand at the unicorn tapestry. "Out of fashion! You will have to pay me to take it away! I won't buy that!" Ella's heart sprang to her throat as she clutched the key to the hidden library, the key she always wore around her neck. The buyer stalked out of the gallery with Heloise remonstrating behind him. Ella did not weep. Every day, as she rose to make porridge and tea, and then went out to work in the garden, or in the fields with Grint, she remembered her father's words "…will you help me? I know it will not be easy…"

One day Ella heard Mrs. Grint screeching at Heloise, "You're not the Lady Davis! You'll not speak to me as if you were! Hannah Grint is long to this land and family, and you're not fit to dig in the Davis garden!" and that was the last time Mrs. Grint came to the manor house. It was hard for Ella. "…suitors will come…" her father had said, so the house must be kept up. But it was hard. Alone. Dear Grint kept working the fields, hiring crews at harvest time. He brought the money to Ella, and she used it for the household, and the lands. Heloise did not dare speak to Grint. He never spoke to her.

Ella stood and smoothed her dress. She stood straight because her mother had. Her hand touched the brush, she brushed her hair back and braided it like her mother had. She shivered, and started down the stair.

~

The blast of a trumpet startled Ella. She had not heard the horse, and Rufus – old and deaf – had not heard either. She hurried from the kitchen, through the small dining hall and down the Long Gallery to the tall door. She pushed it open and blinked in the sudden light. Two mounted men sat in the yard, holding a third horse. A plump man in the prince's livery approached the door. He looked at her a moment, apparently decided she was a servant, and cleared his throat. "An invitation for Lady Davis and her worthy guests to attend at the Prince's Ball on the feast day of St. Peter the Merciful. See that the lady receives it, my dear." He smiled at her, climbed on his horse, and the three cantered away.

"What is this?" came the austere voice of her stepmother. The tall woman took the parchment from Ella's hand, broke the seal, and unfolded the letter. The lines of angst on her face lightened for a moment; she was pretty. Then she whirled and shouted into the gallery, "Girls! Girls, come!"

Ella heard the women chattering excitedly in the small dining hall. She rippled the tapestry and slipped behind it. Her key fit the lock and the door opened soundlessly.

Ella had, as she always did, the sensation of stepping back in time. It had been a chapel, long ago. But for years before Ella's birth, it had been a library – perhaps it was hidden in the tumultuous days when having a proscribed Bible was dangerous. Light poured down, golden dust swam in its beams. Ella stepped to the nearest bookshelf and slid her fingers along the spines of her beloved tomes; she heard the words inside speaking. Most books spoke with her own voice, but some still spoke with her mother's. She touched the Nibelungenlied, and her spirit stirred with the tragic valor of those noble dead; she touched the Psalmodia Germanica, and her heart thrilled with the beauty of the heavenly wedding, and the vision of God's passion for his Beloved.

Oh, to be loved! To be beautiful, and loved!

Ella sighed as she heard, dimly through the door, her stepmother shouting her name. There would be no time to read today. She waited until the gallery was quiet, and then slipped out. As she turned into the kitchen, she almost bumped into Heloise.

"Give it to me! Give me the purse!" She stood tall, flushed, pointing her finger at Ella's nose. The girl stepped back. Heloise followed her. "I know that you hoard money from the crops! Where is it? That belongs to this family! We need it, we must have it now! My daughters will never have a better chance than this! They must appear like women of a noble house, and that is going to cost!"

"But, the hire of the workmen for the harvest – that money must go to pay wages if the crops are to come in, and I have much to buy come autumn and –"

Heloise cut her off with a wave. "Pish! There will be more money after harvest! I know you scrimp every silver scrap! Never, since we came to this house, have you shared a mark of what belongs to us all! Stupid girl! You are waiting for us to go away so you can have all as you like! But I won't see my daughters walk the streets or sing for bread! I will see them well wed while they still bloom! Can't you see that a little spent now will bring much profit to us all? We may yet save this house! The palace of the prince is no place for a lady with no fortune nor father to promote her! The men are dead! I will do what I must! Give me the money!"

Ella turned with her stepmother close behind. They climbed the steps to her chamber and Heloise stood by as she unlocked one of the chests at the foot of her bed. She lifted out the little leather bag with a handful of silver kreuzer, ten heavy groschen, and one old, thin, gold ducat. Was this the *Treasure of the House of Davis*? A hand reached swiftly over her shoulder and snatched the bag. Without another word Heloise hurried from the room. Ella looked after her with sinking heart.

She spoke hardly a word to her stepmother or stepsisters in the days that followed. Trips to the town, and a visit from a tailor and a jeweler followed. Summer bloomed. At last, the day came.

Before dawn Ella began heating water. The three women steeped their bodies in rose-smelling baths, dried, and powdered. They brushed their hair, wiggled into underthings and petticoats, corsets and gowns, and each sat for the others to complete her grooming with scented oils, pins, and clips. They would let Ella have no hand in this. With relief she fled the mess and scents of the women's toilette for the safety of the stable.

Grint had wiped down the carriage at her request. Ella poured the horse a measure of oats as she brushed him. Would a good showing at the prince's ball result in marriages for her stepsisters? Would any of this redeem the Davis Estate? Ella sighed. "Daddy I have done all I could to make the house suitable, and help them find husbands…" The horse raised his head and blew. She kissed his nose, brushed his face, and stepped him in front of the carriage.

The door of the Long Gallery opened. Ella stopped the horse before it. Her stepsisters came out looking lovely with cheeks pink-ed, and adorned with every bit of colored glass Heloise could squeeze out of the jeweler. They were pale under the blush, their breathing shallow. Heloise followed them with a face like a huntress. The three scrambled awkwardly into the carriage, and Heloise took up the reins. She glanced down at Ella and was even pretty as she smiled, "Wish us luck!"

"Good luck." Ella said quietly as they drove away… without her.

IV

Journey

She stood among the blooming
pumpkin vines and looked out over
her ancestral lands. Fields fertile with
crops, the marsh where waterfowl rose with
flashing wings – most of it was mortgaged
now, but she knew its bounds. To the west
and east rose mountains, crags of gray and
blue streaked with snow in the summer
sunshine. Ella looked north where the old
road wound along the river toward a smoky
smudge of the town, and the castle perched
on its hill guarding all. At her feet Rufus

thumped his tail. She knelt to rub his graying ears, warmed from the sun, and he lay back with a sigh.

Ella climbed the stair to her own room. Quickly she packed clothes into a leather knapsack, rolled her mother's heavy woolen cloak and her own blanket together and tied them with a cord. She packed her mother's good leather walking shoes, and shut the door behind her. In the kitchen Ella folded oatcakes into a clean cloth, and took a bottle for water. She lay out three of her favorite knives: the large butcher knife, her bullnose kitchen knife with twins on the blade, and her favorite paring knife (old and worn, but still serviceable) its six-inch blade marked, "Solingen".

At last, she entered the library. Light diffused trickled down from above. Tall, the bookshelves with their memories and mysteries stood around her. Almost, she heard her mother's voice in the quiet. Many times she had lingered there, but not today. Ella set the Froschauer Bible atop the dictionary and folded them both into a cloth. She slid them into her knapsack – bulky now, and stepped down into the Long Gallery. She closed and locked the door behind her, and hung the key on its string around her neck.

In the kitchen she paused to nestle a log into the coals and smoor[11] the fire, and then out into the sweet summer sunshine. She stooped to stroke Rufus. "Goodbye, Friend Hound," she said, and turned her face toward the journey.

Ahead, on the road, a familiar figure limped toward the palace bearing a great

---

[11] Smooring a fire preserves the burning coals by burying them in ash. It is often practical to smoor a fire than to rebuild it.

basket. "Mother Grint!" Ella called, and the old woman stopped and set down her burden. "A favor of you, faithful friend," Ella said, drawing near. "Take Rufus to your hearth, and see that Grint buries him above the creek when his time comes."

Keen gray eyes, young eyes, twinkled in her weathered face. "Lady Davis!" she said, "No, it is her daughter Ella, but Lady Davis herself no less! You seem to have a pack upon ya, and yer feet upon the road!"

"Yes, I've –" Ella began but paused as they heard the clip of hooves. A proud gray horse swept up with a tall, young man on his back. Bright sun gleamed on the gold embroidery of his tabard, and his rich gold hair under a velvet hat. He reined in and looked down at them, his eyes a flash of blue like the sky above, his teeth gleamed white in a sudden smile.

"Fair damsels, I give you good greeting and God's blessing on this saint's day!" Mrs. Grint nodded her head, Ella blushed and dropped a small curtsey. "Where are you going, so burdened?" He asked.

"We're bound to sell these vegetables up in the town," Mrs. Grint said with the reserved politeness of a proud commoner answering a noble.

"And you, maiden, who are you, and where are you going, laden with a pack?" His gaze swept Ella approvingly.

"Sir, I am named Ella, and I am seeking honorable employment."

"It is a blessed day for us all three!" he exclaimed. "I am Gilbert! Page and Companion of the Prince!" He sought in his purse and drew out a little sack of coins which he handed down to Mrs. Grint. She opened the pouch, peered inside, and gasped. Gilbert laughed. "This day my dear Prince hosts a celebration for all the nobility of his lands, and tonight, a royal ball! We will need all the quality vegetables we can buy, and our chef, Jacques, the worthy Frank, requires more hands in his kitchen!

"Have you worked in a kitchen pretty one?" he smiled down at Ella. She nodded. He laughed. "Well then, when your grandmother deliverers her vegetables to the palace kitchen, you deliver yourself to Jacques and tell him Gilbert the Page sent you! Be warned, you must be ready to hustle! But be cheered! You will see me again! Farewell, fair ones!" and with a shake of the reins he was off.

Mrs. Grint looked at Ella as she gazed down the road after the departing horseman. "And the heat of your blushing is worse than the sun!" she grunted.

"What?" Ella asked.

"You'd better take a slow breath or you'll faint on the road; then I'll needs carry you, and the basket, and the pack all three back to the Manor! And the prince won't get his vegetables."

"He spoke kindly to us! He was so polite and smiled at us! He bought your basket! He was so... gracious, and in the Prince's livery!" Ella glanced up to the sky.

Mrs. Grint snorted. "Sometimes you're yer father's daughter more than yer mother's!" Ella looked a question. "Do you think he was smiling at you?"

"Mmm... Yes?" Ella said.

"My dear, Mother Grint was not always Mother Grint. Once I was a comely lass, and in those days many a soldier and noble traveled this road. Nowadays young folks think they know what their elders don't — but how do you think you all got here?" Ella looked blank. "Ella dear, you're not the first young thing to hear a compliment from that man — who is nearer his thirtieth year than his twentieth — and he did not pay me a six-month wage because he needs a basket of weeds. I say that man did not see you!"

"But Mother Grint, he spoke with us! He asked my name, he sent me to — "

"Yes he sent ya to the palace! I heard that, and said ye'd be seeing more of him. He thought he bought you for a sack of silver! That man was talking to the mound of red and gold you wear on yer head, and those blue eyes like yer mother's, and to your pretty face and blossoming maidenly figure — and maybe he's got sense to do so — but he never spoke to *you*! I say he never saw ya!" The old woman smiled, but her eyes were hard and earnest.

Ella reached out and took her hand. "Then what should I do?"

Mother Grint squeezed it and said, "Remember that I see *you* my dear. Remember that the Good God watches over ya. St. Christopher and the Virgin go with you, travel ya must. To work at the palace is no bad thing. But there are many kinds of folk in the world in every station, and it is true that wealth and ease bring out the best in few. *This*," she tossed and caught the bag of coins, "bought *that*," she pointed to the basket, "and has nothing to do with you!"

Ella put her arms around her friend and kissed her brow. Her eyes welled up with tears. "Farewell! And thank you, thank you! Thank you, for everything!" She stooped then, and lifted the basket. "I will be taking this with me and save you the walk!"

"Blessings on you dear child!" the old woman choked, and turned away.

V

Kitchen

The sun was two hours past noon, and hot, when Ella trudged through the herb garden and into the big kitchen of the prince's castle. She set down the heavy basket, took the dipper from a bucket of water, and drank deeply. The palace bustled with servants hurrying on errands.

Ella called cautiously, "Jacques! Delivery! New help here!"

A moment later a flushed and whiskered face under a tall, white hat peeked out from behind an oven. "And that's the delivery, and you're the help?" the man asked in a French accent. Ella smiled and nodded. "Well stow your pack, missie, wash your hands, and get you to preparing what you've brought!" and he disappeared.

The great clock said 1:30 in the morning when at last Ella and the other kitchen staff sat down to eat. Ella was so tired she could have slept with her face on the table, but she was ravenously hungry and giddy with excitement. Sweet summer air flowed in from the garden, and strains of sweeter music wafted from the ballroom. Scullions and cooks laughed and joked in three languages. The food was better than Ella had ever tasted. At last, she picked up her pack and followed the other women to the dormitory. And that was her first day at the palace.

With the dawn she was up and working again. What a joy for her to work and learn! And what a pleasure to eat such food, for the palace servants ate as well as the prince, and Ella was still a growing girl. Jacques took a liking to his new help, and she to him. True, the Frenchman laughed loudly at his own stories, but he was as respectful as any knight to those under him, and a master of the culinary craft.

And there was Gilbert. The day after the ball he was there with flowers to welcome her to the palace. He suggested a walk after her evening work was done, but Ella was weary. Gilbert was back the next day "Helen," he said, "this day is almost as beautiful as you! My horse will carry two! Come with me to the cool shade along the riverside, we will celebrate the day!" Ella smiled, and with her knife gestured to the mound of potatoes around her. Gilbert winked and turned away with a laugh. An hour later, as Ella carried a load of peelings to the compost, she heard a squealing giggle and glimpsed the golden-haired man trotting by on a gray horse. A serving woman sat on the horse's rump with her arms about the man's waist. A wiser Ella went back to her peeling.

The prince's palace was a wonderful place. Ella was thrilled to hear the music, and see the horses and fine clothes of the noble persons who dwelt or visited there. Once the prince's aged mother spoke kindly to her. Always there was friendly, (and sometimes less than friendly,) banter among the staff. The kitchen labor was relentless, but Ella was better fed and better rested than she had been since childhood.

Gilbert persisted. Some days Jacques met him outside the kitchen to say that Ella was away. Sometimes Jacques would call her or send for her when Gilbert had caught her in conversation in the midst of her work. Sometimes the other servants would warn her and she would be scarce, but several times each week, and sometimes each day, he would come looking for her with an invitation to 'slip away'.

~

Jacques looked sad as she entered the kitchen one morning. "Ella *ma belle enfant*,[12] it pains my heart, but it is best for you if I write you a letter of introduction and send you away. No *ma chérie*, [13] don't be sad, you have done no wrong – I'd rather have you than the rest of my staff! But the palace is not the best place for you anymore, I think. You have noticed Gilbert – he is easy to notice – and I see that you would rather not be walking with him in the moonlight and that is because you are a good girl. Gilbert, well, he is a rather a man who likes himself better than anyone. You are not the first girl he smiles on, and most little girls smile back, but not you. You carry yourself like a lady, and perhaps he likes that, and I think that is why he keeps coming. *Ma chérie*, forgive me

---

[12] *Ma belle enfant* – 'my beautiful child' *French.*
[13] *Ma chérie* – 'my dear' *French.*

for speaking plainly – his interest will not long outlast your consent."

Jacques spread his hands, "But there is only so much I can do to keep him away. If he were a stable boy – oui! – or even a man-at-arms I'd send him off! For the Chef is second only to the Prince! But with Gilbert it is different. He is the prince's companion; he is like family. Like *Family*!" he repeated meaningfully.

Ella nodded.

"And so *ma chérie*, I fear you must be going, but you have wages coming, and I will write a letter introducing you to my brother Pierre who keeps him a hunting chateau in the mountains. He has a busy house and his own daughters gone and married. He will be glad of the help! And it will be a safe place for you *ma Ingénue Adeline.*[14]" He smiled at her kindly and sniffed. "Now be kind to me and lend me your knife, and I will make a visit to the cobbler and the treasury. You be good and pack food to last a four-day tramp, and

---

[14] Ma Ingénue Adeline – 'virtuous, noble girl' French.

don't be shy for the prince has plenty in his larder and can eat none of it without me!"

By the time Ella had packed clothes and provisions, Jacques was back. "And here *ma colombe*[15] is your serpent's tooth like the Scriptures say," and he gave back her own knife deep in a new scabbard of fine leather. "The cobbler made this for you. He dropped the shoe in his hand when I told him you were for the road, and he made this for you – sometimes a girl needs more than a sweet smile to get her way! And here are your wages. No *ma colombe*, do not count them until you are safe to my brother's chateau! Best if no one knows you have silver – none but an old friend dearly trusted! If you must spend money by the way, show but one piece, part with it dear as the moon! A queen uses silver as a battering ram to open close-locked gates, but that is a play for a princess older than you! And this, best of all, is a letter for Pierre *mon cher frère* [16] from his Jacques.

---

[15] *Ma colombe* – 'my dove' *French.*
[16] *mon cher frère* – 'my dear brother' *French.*

42

"And now *ma fille,*[17] go! Go before I weep upon you, and how I will keep this kitchen without your sweet self I do not know, for you are worth more than all the others!" And the pride ran down his cheeks.

Ella stepped up on a stool there and kissed his red brow. *"Grand-père Jacques, Dieu vous bénisse.*[18]"

He wept.

She clasped his hand for a moment, took up her pack and turned light-hearted toward the door, and the road.

---

[17] *Ma fille* – 'my daughter' *French.*
[18] *Grand-père Jacques, Dieu vous bénisse* – 'God bless you Grandfather Jacques' *French.*

VI

Traveling Companions

S he heard them singing in the gloaming. Rounding a bend she saw a blur of white wimples and recognized the *Miserere*, the 51st Psalm that Mother Grint used to sing. As Ella came humming behind them, one of the Carmelites turned and smiled at her. "Are you traveling, little sister? We are just coming to our place of rest, will you stay with us?"

Ella thought of the dark road ahead. She had planned to walk another mile before seeking a hidden place to sleep, and she had planned to start out again before Lauds. It was a long, four-day walk from the palace to Pierre's Mountain Chateau… But the welcome was genuine, and she would be safer with the women. "I would be glad to!" Ella said.

The little wayside chapel was an ancient place, its level floor fragrant with the stalks of beaten lavender. There were no fleas. The Carmelites insisted on sharing their simple fare with Ella, and soon she was asleep.

Singing awakened her. Ella sat up stiffly and rubbed her eyes. The nuns were all outside the little chapel, singing into the dawn. Ella hummed a psalm of her own as she brushed her hair, straightened her clothes, and rolled her bed. Her belly growled and as she was digging a morsel out of her pack the mendicants came chattering in. "We have broken fast with prayer!" one of the sisters announced, "Now, let us be on our way."

Ella closed her knapsack and joined the throng as they followed the mile of winding footpath which took them back to the highway. She wondered if perhaps she should turn aside and let the good sisters go ahead without her, but she grudged the lost time – resting at the chapel had already added two unnecessary miles to a long trip – so she kept pace with the Carmelites, and together they joined the road. "Are you on pilgrimage, dear child?" a kindly nun asked.

"I am traveling," Ella answered. "How did you come to take vows?"

The older woman smiled. "Sisters come to the order by many doors, some as children, some after the death of a husband, or to avoid one!" She laughed. "I was restless! My older sisters were all married with many children, and I loved them, but I wanted to do more, to travel and see God's world!"

Were not nuns cloistered? Ella wondered. "And have you traveled much?"

"Oh yes! Twice I have been to Rome. Now we go to Toulouse, and then on to Compiègne. I have learned medicine, and to read and write the Latin and French! I have even met sisters from England! Have you considered a holy order?"

"I haven't," Ella admitted. "Tell me of your vocation." Ella wanted to keep the conversation going, and to distract herself from growing hunger. "What do you treasure most?"

"Oh, the purity of life," the nun smiled. "Everything we do is holy to the honor of the Virgin and her Holy Son. And I love to teach the younger women –"

At the head of the column someone began to sing, "Lord God, the maker of all things…" and the nun beside Ella joined the midday hymn. The women stopped and stood together. When the Sext prayer was complete, they began to pray for provision of food. Ella stood uncomfortably hungry and awkward as the women prayed. At last, she opened her knapsack and took out the traveling rations she had packed so carefully. "Please share this with me," she offered. With murmurs of thanks the nuns accepted, and sat down in the shade to partake.

VII

Potter's Grotto

At the crossroads the women went singing toward the south, and Ella continued on her way. "My pack is lighter," Ella reasoned, "and I have fasted before." Ahead, three figures were struggling on the road. She stopped and stared. Two boys, small boys, seemed to be wrestling with something, with a donkey, heaving a load onto its back. No sooner did the bundle go up than it toppled and the sticks scattered. "Here lads," Ella called, "Let me take a hand!" The grubby boys looked at her hopefully, their cheeks smeared with frustrated tears. The donkey's ears drooped in relief. Ella lay out the sticks and wove the cord through, separating the load into four connected bundles. This she laid over the donkey's back and lashed under his belly.

Apparently, the boys had been wood-gathering for quite some time, for there were two more piles of sticks at the forest's edge. Ella glanced up and down the road, but there was no forester, indeed no one at all in view, and evening was drawing on. When Ella began to lay out the sticks, one of the boys said, "Don't mix them!" She looked a question at him. "Don't mix them," he repeated. "Mommy has to have the fir and the oak separate!" Ella nodded and made two bundles of the remaining sticks. She hoisted one atop her own knapsack, and the boys, Peter and Paul, took up the other and led the way. Ella and the donkey followed.

Lights, warm and friendly, glowed from a window in the long, low, white cottage. Two hive-shaped structures loomed beside a workshop, barely visible in the gloaming. The creek's voice, and the chirrrip of frogs sang in the little canyon. The boys ran shouting down the path as the cottage door swung open. Orange light spilled out, silhouetting a woman who knelt to clasp the children. The donkey turned aside to his stable. The boys ran to loosen his load, brush him, and turn him free to graze. Ella set down her bundle of sticks.

The boys hurried toward the house, and she followed them. "You have helped my sons, good neighbor," the woman's voice was kind. Tired, but kind. "Please honor us by sharing our meal."

"I thank you. The honor is mine," Ella said, and stopped her curtsey just in time. She set down her knapsack and looked around the cottage. The woman took one of the three bowls from the board and quietly poured half its soup into a fourth bowl, topped them both with hot water from an earthen vessel by the hearth, and turned to the table. In the dim light from the hearthfire, Ella saw her smiling.

"Blessings to you traveler. Welcome to the home of Peter the Potter. I am Patty, and these are our sons Paul and Peter. Alas, their father has passed, but soon they will be men grown. Already they work like it." The boys sat straighter before their bowls. Ella took a place at the board table. Her hostess sat, and passed the loaf.

Ella ate slowly, savoring every morsel. It had been many miles since noon, and she was glad of the soup – thin though it was. The boys slurped their supper, washed, and went to bed. Ella helped Patty rinse the bowls and wooden spoons, and then the women sat beside the embers with mugs of sideritis[19] tea. She felt herself relaxing in the dim, quiet warmth of the cottage. Patty spoke. "Ella, I do not mean to pry, but I ask as a mother: why are you traveling alone?"

The embers blurred before Ella's eyes. Her voice choked. She heard someone

---

[19] Sideritis Tea, or Shepherd's Tea, has been brewed in central Europe and the Mediterranean regions since ancient times.

crying, and was surprised to find it was herself. Gentle arms wrapped around her, she put her head on Patty's shoulder and wept. A long time later Patty poked the coals and settled a knot of wood into them, raking the ash over. Ella was composed. "My parents are in the churchyard not far from the house where I was born. I worked for a time in the prince's kitchen. A man there – he had intentions for me – so Jacques the chef wrote me a letter of introduction to his brother's chateau in the mountains. I am carrying the letter, hoping for work there." Patty sat silent, holding Ella's hand.

"Do you have any people?" Ella shook her head. "Do you know the house you are going to?" Patty worried.

"No, but Jacques was good to me – to all the servants – and he assured me that his brother is a decent man." Ella took a steadying breath and smiled. "Long ago my father's people were driven out of Britannia by Saxon invaders. We made the mountains of Snowdon our fortress, and were free there for a thousand years. Our ancestor David followed Owain Glyndŵr;[20] David survived and fled with his family beyond the reach of the English kings. Like many nobles of Cymru, his grandson became an officer in the armies of Imperium Christianum, was awarded lands and made a lord of the empire. But we never went back to Britain. Father told me these tales sometimes… Now we speak no Gymraeg, and have no people there." Ella breathed a ragged sigh. "Many women have been alone, have started again…"

"It is hard to be alone," Patty spoke softly. Gently she patted Ella's back as the younger woman slept.

Morning filled the vale with birdsong. Ella awoke to the shouts of the boys outside. Patty smiled at her as she grilled cakes at the hearth. As the women munched cakes and drank their re-warmed tea, Patty

---

[20] Owain Glyndŵr Prince of Wales, 1359 -1415, was a knight, statesman, and general. He outfought and outlived Henry the IV of England, presided over a free Welsh Parliament, and planned the establishment of Welsh universities, courts, and a national church. He was repeatedly attacked by the English, was defeated in 1409, and his followers scattered.

told how Peter's family had lived and worked in this valley for many generations. They held long-standing permissions[21] to cut wood and dig clay from the creek. For generations they held a booth of honor at two 'messe' – important regional fairs.[22] "He sickened and died suddenly," Patty said. "Now I am learning the potter's craft and making inventory to sell at the fairs. If I can hold on, just for a few years, until the boys are old enough, we will keep their inheritance…" She sighed.

"Is there work for two more hands?" Ella wondered.

~

Work enough for two weary backs, four hands, and four legs! All day the women dug in the creek, mounding clay on the sled, and helping the donkey drag it to the pits behind

---

[21] In Europe, natural resources were controlled by the nobility; mining, forestry, and inland fishing required special permissions which were sometimes granted, sometimes bought, and sometimes inherited.

[22] Annual fairs were a cornerstone of Europe's medieval and renaissance economy. People traveled to buy and sell goods, and conclude business agreements. Fairs were sometimes authorized and protected by nobles, or town committees.

the workshop. "And this," Patty gasped as her spade struck the sled and the clump of clay broke free, "is the reason Peter's ancestors were settled here! This white clay is treasured above all others for its smoothness and color. Peter could throw a pot so fine that light would come through it!"

"Uhhhh," Ella agreed, as her wooden spade came up loaded, and dripping.

Patty clunked another glump on the sled. The donkey sighed. The sun fell behind the mountains. Cold air flowed up the creek.

Ella shivered and heaved. Clay clung to the blade. Every scoop was a labor. The boys were back at the house already. Ella's belly grumbled. She clamped her teeth over her complaints and strained at the spade.

Dusk. At last Patty spoke to the donkey. He set into his collar as the women levered their spades and heaved on the sled, it moved, they pushed, he pulled, it moved. Ella fell, but Patty kept the sled going up onto the level ground and on toward the house. Ella picked up her spade and followed.

Morning light found them cutting and mixing, kneading and blending the clay with water and a variety of sands and soils stored in the workshop. Ella closed her eyes and stepped, stepped, stepped. She felt Peter, or Paul, splash water into the low pit she trod, but she did not look up. She kept stepping.

At last, they crawled out of the pits and washed in the creek. Ella fell asleep while eating dinner. Peter woke her, "Mommy has gone back to work." Ella staggered up and went out to find Patty. Afternoon lasted a year. Everyone was asleep by twilight. In the morning Patty sent Peter and Ella out with the donkey for fuel while she and Paul mixed the precious clay.

The next day, Patty spun the wheel.

Ella had risen early, cooked porridge, and made herb tea while the others slept. After breaking fast, Peter and Paul went fishing along the creek, and Patty led the way to the workshop. A whole family of potters could work there together. One long wall was lined with shelves awaiting an inventory. By a window there stood a wheel. A thin ceramic disk sat cleated on the wheel's circular top. Others rested on a shelf. The wheel itself was supported by a table of polished wood; a shaft from the wheel passed through the table, and was pegged into a hole in a wide stone disk poised horizontally above the floor. A stool waited nearby.

Patty took a clump of clay, rolled it between wet hands, and set it in the center of the wheel. She sat and, with her foot, pushed the stone disk. She kept it spinning and the wheel spun too, faster and faster. Patty dipped her hands in the water, reached out, and touched the clay. Time stopped. Ella's world became the gentle creak of the wheel, and the whisper of Patty's hands on damp clay. Up from the wheel sprang a vessel, graceful and undulating, smooth and tapering in the neck, flaring to a lip Patty trimmed with a flake of flint. She cleaned the clay, slowed the wheel with her foot, and sat back. Patty turned to Ella and smiled.

Morning light had marched across the room to afternoon. Ella realized that she was hungry and stiff. Patty gently turned the wheel, looking at the vessel, touching it occasionally to make changes Ella could not see. She lifted the disk – the 'bat' – on which the tender clay rested, and set it with the vessel on a shelf in the afternoon light.

Patty washed. In silence they walked toward the cottage.

Ella's mind was in the Long Gallery at Davis Manor, looking at the portraits of her ancestors with their weapons, and horses, and hounds. She thought of her mother and the library. How could generations of her family live alongside this enchantment, and never know it? The deeds of her house were insignificant beside the gentle magic of Patty's hands raising a bit of soil into a thing of elegance, use, and beauty. She realized that Patty had been speaking "…when all are ready the boys will stoke the kiln for firing. It must be hot to bake the glaze and become strong, but not too hot or the clay will melt!" She smiled up to the sky. "We will fill our booth! Won't Peter be proud?! The clay threw just as I had hoped. We will keep the cottage, and the kilns, and my grandchildren will play here!" She laughed, stretched her arms high, and, to Ella's astonishment, rolled a cartwheel! Peter and Paul raced up from the creek and rolled cartwheels too.

Ella had not tumbled since she was a girl. After Heloise came, Ella never played again. She watched between laughter and tears as the Potters rolled and laughed around her. "Try, try!" little Peter insisted, tugging at her hands, and Ella did. They rolled and laughed in the grass until evening. The two young women and the two little boys did not eat much, but they ate together, and were glad.

All the next day Patty worked at the wheel. One vessel joined another on the shelves to await firing: bowls and pitchers, cups, chalices, urns, even amphoras (made of two joined pieces, and flattened on the bottom to stand). Patty used clay from different pits, mixed with several sands and types of grog to make vessels of various colors, or for different purposes.

On the third day Patty placed a lump of white clay on the wheel. It had been mixed with a very fine, white power of baked ceramic. Patty smiled and gestured. Ella sat with a fluttering heart and pushed the stone disk with her foot. As the wheel began to spin, Ella imagined a chalice rising from the precious clay. Her hands would transform the lump into a thing of beauty! She dipped her hands as she had seen Patty do, reached out as she had seen Patty do, and at her touch the clay leapt from the wheel and rolled on the floor! Ella cried in dismay. Patty laughed, put the lump in a bucket, and set a fresh ball of clay on the wheel. This time she took Ella's hands in her own and guided them. Four thumbs dented the lump; sixteen fingers supported it. The clay narrowed and rose. Patty stepped away, and Ella was alone with the spinning wheel and the clay. Where was the magic? She tried to replicate the care and authority of Patty's hands on the clay... but the mass before her bulbled lumpy and asymmetrical, she sought to thin it when suddenly a hole appeared in one side, and the vessel collapsed under her touch! Choking with anger and shame, she dragged her foot hard on the stone disk. The wheel stopped. With hot tears Ella took the lump and rolled it, patting as she had seen her friend do, and set it again in the center of the wheel. It spun. She dipped, and touched.

At twilight Patty lifted the bat and set Ella's humble cup on the shelf beside the vessels she had made. They walked to the cottage as frogs sang. An owl flickered by, white in the gloaming. "Peter and I were married seven years," Patty said quietly. "I liked to spin the wheel while rocking the cradle. I have seen my man throw thousands of pots. After his brother and nephew died, he used to hire a neighbor lad to dig clay in the creek..." Ella nodded, silent. Yes, Patty had years of practice, but Ella's heart told her that there was more: Patty's hands and heart held a creative power that was not in hers.

~

Patty spent days glazing her handiwork. She loaded the kiln and carefully stacked wood so the fire would draw and burn hot. Early in the morning, she started the fire. All day she tended the kiln, watching the coals, judging the heat, adding wood.

Ella roamed along the creek with the boys, fishing in the morning, and gathering fuel in the afternoon. She found a dry ash sapling standing slim and straight in a grove. She uprooted it and carried it home with her load. As the soup simmered, she trimmed off the twigs with her knife, and smoothed the knots. By suppertime she had a straight walking stick with a knob at the top where the roots had been. It was almost as long as her arms' span, and smooth, a staff fit for a pilgrim.

Patty came in late, smelling like the kiln, and smiling. "The pottery is cooling now. I fired your cup." Ella smiled, but she was abashed. It had not been the chalice she imagined; in the end she had settled for a simple cup, such as a man and woman might share at table. It had been smooth, and thin, but the top was not perfect. Simple, but not inelegant.

At last the kiln was cool, and Ella watched Patty pack her finished goods for the fair. "I see that you have made a staff..." Patty said.

"Yes. I will go while the weather is still fine for traveling."

"You have been a blessing to us, to the boys – and you have been a friend to me..." Patty smiled sadly.

Perhaps if Ella had discovered an aptitude for the wheel... But she had none. Now there was enough clay in the pits to last for a long time, and fuel for several more firings. Ella knew what the larder held; it might have fed another worker... but it was not enough to feed a guest.

Ella was packed and ready with the dawn. Patty held her for a long time in a mother's embrace, kissed her brow, and pressed a bag of provisions into her hand. "For your journey," she said. Ella nestled it in her knapsack, took up her staff, and stepped out into the morning.

VIII

Mountain Pasture

The road climbed through green oak groves, and ran down draws where ash trees shed dun leaves. A clean, crisp promise of autumn hung in the air.

Midmorning sun poured light over the slope as Ella rested on an outcropping of stone, gazing back over the folds of land hiding the potter's valley. Ahead the mountains rose blue. She opened her knapsack. Small apples smiled up from the bag Patty had prepared. There were also three, thin-baked cakes of oat flour.

Underneath was something wrapped in a rag. Ella unrolled it. The cup! But not as she had last seen it. Ella had formed the vessel of clean clay; glaze and fire had transmuted it into a thing of beauty, translucent with brimming sunlight. She breathed deeply, smelling the kiln, feeling the cold creek, hearing the laughter of her friends... With a sigh, and a smile, she carefully, carefully stowed the cup in her pack.

Afternoon grew hot as Ella trudged higher into the foothills. Sweat trickled into her eyes. She looked up from the road and saw a grove of dark cedars on the slope above. *That looks like a good place to rest,* she thought, *shaded, sheltered. I can read for a while, make a fire tonight, and start before the light comes tomorrow. I suppose that will put me at Pierre's in two days — one with food and one with fasting — like a good pilgrim.* Ella laughed to herself as she turned off the road and followed a dim trail up the forested slope.

The grove's deep shade was inviting, but a sudden sound startled her. Branches shook. Ella caught her breath and grasped her knife. She saw a flash of white in the shadow, and heard a gasping bleat. She hurried forward where the cedar bows swept to the ground. Trapped under one of them was a small sheep, the ground torn from its struggling. Ella heaved up the bough and wedged her staff under it, then she grasped the sheep's legs and dragged it out into the sunlight.

"Floushe! Floushe!" Ella heard a child calling.

"Here!" Ella answered, "I have your sheep!"

A small, dark-haired girl came bounding through the underbrush. "Oh, you silly!" she said, kneeling by the sheep as it struggled to rise.

"It was trapped here —" Ella offered. Her eyes strayed to the child's dirty, tattered woolen dress, her grubby limbs…

"Oh yes!" the girl interrupted, "Floushe likes to rub on the boughs, I have found her trapped here before. Brother Etzel says that she doesn't have any sense!"

"I am called Ella. What is your name?"

"I am Ida, the Shepherd's Daughter. All the sheep in this pasture are mine – well, they are mine and Dafid's, but he is just five, so Papa says that I am in charge. Sometimes Dafid doesn't do what I tell him to, and Etzel says I should stop tattling and just do the work. But I think he switched Dafid once, because after that he was better for a whole week! But now he has a sling and I think he is going to hurt one of our sheep – he isn't slinging at them, but he is just slinging a lot of rocks. Where is your home? Are you a grownup?"

Ella laughed. "I am a grownup! And I do not have a home, I am traveling to work. I think your little sheep will walk now, shall we take her and you to your home?" Ida smiled, and the two went together, following the young sheep.

"Papa says that our fold is old. He says it was here before the Old Roam-Mans. Me and Dafid keep sheep here all summer, and the winter too. Papa's other shepherds take their sheep way up the mountain in the summertime, and down to valley come winter, but we stay here because there is grass in the forest and the sheep like it and our sheep are the special sheep cuz they are older or younger than the others."

"Hmmm," Ella observed.

"And Etzel brings us supplies and I do all the cooking because I am oldest. Dafid is only five but he says he is bravest because he bees a boy. But our fold is the best one because it has the long shed for the sheep." She pointed past a stream and up the rise to a stone wall topped with dry bramble. A hill, tall and tree-clad, loomed beyond the fold. A mile of rising, grassy pasture ended in dark shadow and rocky scree at the mountain's foot. White sheep came bobbing down the slope, following the tiny figure of a dark-haired boy.

He met them at the fold and stared at Ella. She smiled at him, but his grubby face stayed solemn. He took Ida's hand and whispered, "Etzel will be mad!"

The sun set behind the mountains. Sheep trickled past them into the fold, and Ida dragged the gate closed. Once it had been stout wicker, now many laths were broken, and the bramble winding through it hung dead and dry. The gate looked tired. The fold looked tired. Sheep gathered at the far end under a long, thatched shelter built against the wall. Closer to them, another, more substantial shelter also leaned against the stone of the fold. Two upright posts held a lintel, and rough branch rafters ran back to the wall. These in turn were crossed with sticks, and a heavy thatch covered all. One side was sheltered from the wind by a dry wicker screen. Two small bedrolls lay close to the smoored ashes of a fire. "You children are alone?" Ella wondered, "Will your father come tonight?"

Ida shook her head. "Papa has to work. He has lots of work because we have lots of sheep. Our big shepherds – the grownups – are at those pastures," she waved a hand vaguely at the mountain, "and Grim the hunter is there. Brother Etzel will come with the cart and bring food because he always is going round with a cart and food because he has to take food to the big shepherds! We will see him tomorrow or soon I think."

"He will bring ham!" Dafid declared, and clamped his mouth shut as if surprised to hear his own voice.

Ida stirred up the fire, and Dafid fetched water from the stream. Ella took out her cakes and apples. Ida shaved dry meat into a small caldron as the water heated. The children were glad to eat Ella's food, and glad to share their soup with her. As evening's chill settled on the land, Ella opened her Bible and read from the story of Saul the Benjamite and David the shepherd who became king.

"Dafid had a sling?!" Little Dafid was incredulous. His reserve forgotten, he cuddled close to Ella's side, gazing at the pictures in the Froschauer Bible.

"*A king he became, but first a shepherd with a sling.*" Ella smiled at the little lad's wrinkled brow. "King David was learned, even when he was a boy; he knew the Law of God and made songs which he sang to his sheep under the stars. But now it is time for kings and ladies to be sleeping."

Ida smoored the fire, and Ella wrapped herself in her blanket and cloak. The children lay down, one on either side of her. When she awoke in the morning, they were both snuggled close to her, sleeping sweetly.

Ella went out with the children and the flock that day. She listened to Ida's chatter, and watched Dafid cast rocks from his sling. She caught a fish in the stream, much to the delight of the little shepherds. Their flock was small, the sheep old, or weak, or young. They were docile, and came at the children's call. In the evening Ella again read to Ida and Dafid while the fish seasoned their soup. After supper the littles snuggled against Ella and fell asleep. She lay, staring long at the stars, thinking and praying. By morning she knew.

About midday Dafid gave a shout, Ida leapt up. "Etzel is coming!"

Ella saw a lone man behind a barrow, toiling up the path toward the fold. Dafid hopped beside him. Ida raced to greet him. Ella followed slowly.

"Ella is our friend!" Ida announced, tugging her hand, "She has a book and caught a fish!" Etzel was not tall; his well-made woolen garments were worn and dusty. Ella saw his dark eyes register her appearance, and the circumstance; she saw doubt there. But he greeted her politely and continued with his barrow up to the fold.

Ella followed him, thinking quickly, weighing the small bag of silver Jacques had paid her. Etzel unpacked his barrow and gave a package to each child. The cloth coverings unrolled into long woolen scarves. Wrapped inside each was a woolen cap. While the children squealed with delight and put on their new things, Etzel turned toward Ella. The look on his face said that he, too, had been thinking, and had come to a conclusion.

Ella struck first. "Your father has the lease of these lands from Prince Antoine's steward, I think? My father, Lord Charles

Davis, drew sword with him in Vienna[23] when the horse had the mastery over the Turks. He carried the prince when he was wounded in the onslaught." The young shepherd was taller than she, but her father's steel was in her voice. Etzel's cap came off. "I am traveling this twelvemonth, for reasons of my own, and it pleases me to stay the winter with these children on this mountain." She saw the muscles in his face tighten. "They are wintering here with the sheep, yes?" He nodded, and drew breath to speak, but Ella went on. "I would have you buy what I need and deliver it to me here." She held out the bag. He extended his hand and Ella poured the silver into it, dropping the bag atop the money in his palm. She spoke out the list she had compiled: oats and salt, tea and dry meat, and added, "There will be enough left to buy a decent

---

[23] Battle of Vienna, 1683: The Ottoman Empire besieged Vienna with an army numbering 150,000 - 300,000 warriors with sappers, engineers, cannon, food, and treasure. Half the defenders of Vienna died in the desperate siege, but even after the walls were breached, they refused to surrender. The Christian States of Europe assembled an army of 70,000 - 80,000, routed the Turks, and saved the city.

mule. You may have the use of him while I tarry here."

Etzel looked at the silver in his hand. His expression hardened and his eyes raised to hers. He looked at her a long time, searchingly, appraisingly. "My lady, forgive my asking, but are you in hiding? Will your presence here bring danger to my brother and sister?"

Ella shook her head. "I am in no danger, nor do I bring any. However, you may tell no one my name, and the fewer people who know of my presence, the better. I am on a journey, and I am in no hurry to reach its end. It pleases me to winter here."

Etzel's hand closed on the money and he made a small bow. "I will do as you ask."

He did.

~

Autumn came cold and bright to the mountains. Larch trees blazed golden in the frosty air. Starlight glowed bright as a reading lamp over Ella and the children as she sat with the Bible in her lap, sharing again the deeds of David the King, and his champions. Ida and Dafid nestled near. Ella's finger traced the page as she read, and both the children spoke the words with her, their voices rising and falling with the cadence of the tale. Dafid gazed at the fire, but Ida watched the page.

Etzel brought Ella supplies packed on the mule she had purchased. He showed her how to secure the grain against rats and squirrels. When they followed the sheep out to graze on the slopes above the forest, Etzel walked with them. The children ran ahead and Ella laughed to see them. She lifted her walking stick. "Shepherd's staff!" she smiled.

Etzel nodded. "The children will keep the sheep to the high benches as long as they can. All this," he gestured to the grass carpeting the forest, "they will save for winter. The sheep will forage under these trees when the snow is deep."

"They are young to be here, on the Mountain with the sheep…" Ella ventured.

"Lady Davis, they are old enough! For a hundred generations my family has lived here – on these slopes. Our men wore wolf scars as their battle honors! When there was hunger, our women went without to feed the children and the men." Etzel's voice was hard.

"I did not mean – " Ella began, but he cut her off.

"Their grandfather, my grandfather was manumitted[24] when my father was an infant." They walked in silence as the words sunk in. Etzel's father was born a serf. "He became first a wage-laborer for his old Lord, and then was made Steward of Flocks, and allowed to graze sheep of his own. In time, he bought the lord's flocks, and leased these lands."

There is honor in such a thing...." Ella said tentatively.

"Perhaps, but there is not always *food*," Etzel's tone was grim. "Have you ever been hungry?"

---

[24] European serfs were like slaves, but bound to the land, owing agricultural service to the lord of the estate on which they lived, and subject to his laws. Manumission changed a serf and all his decedents into free persons. Manumission was sometimes granted, sometimes bought.

Ella lifted her chin and her jaw tightened. Her father, hands hardened by the plow, carrying home turnips with a smile. Fish cooking on the kitchen hearth. Oats. Months of porridge with shreds of dried meat. The calf her father slaughtered every year to feast to the harvesters, a hogshead of beer, a barrel of wine – her father laughing with the men, speaking kindly to their children, sipping the wine in his goblet, eating none of the feast. The icy cold of the solar in winter driving them to the kitchen. But no, never real hunger. She was aware of Etzel's eyes upon her. She did not meet his gaze. She shook her head slightly.

His voice was gentler. "Lady Davis, my father is a good man who knows sheep, and grass, weaving, and markets – though perhaps he trusts too easily. He works harder and walks farther than I do. My sisters and mother labor every day at the wheel and loom. If plague does not take us, or wolves take the sheep, and if the Westphalia Peace holds, my children will sleep in beds instead of in the hills like my little sister and brother, and myself. Perhaps my grandchildren will have leisure to read…"

"You have many children?" Ella grasped at a chance to turn the conversation. She was rewarded by a dark flush creeping up Etzel's throat.

He shook his head. "None. Nor a wife." Etzel called a farewell to Ida and Dafid, and tuned back down the mountain.

One afternoon Ella set the Bible in Ida's lap. "Please read to us," she encouraged, "point at the words, and say them." Haltingly, and then with increasing fluency, Ida recited the stories she knew by heart. Then they read other passages, Ella speaking each word until they reached a word Ida knew, and then the girls reading together. They read again in the evening. Dafid slept, and Ella and Ida read on as moonglow lit the peaks around them. Far off on the mountain, wolves howled. Closer, an owl hooted.

"But what does this word mean?" Ida wondered.

"I don't know" Ella admitted, "but I will share a special secret my mother had for learning." She took out the dictionary and, opening the book, they turned pages until they found the word.

"Can I read it?" Ida wondered, looking at the pictures.

Ella left the book in Ida's lap, tucked sleeping Dafid's blanket tightly around him, and settled herself in for sleep.

The next afternoon, Ida watched Ella wash her clothes in the cold stream. "Why do you do this every week? They will only become dirty again. And why do you always wash them on Woden's-Day?[25]"

Ella smiled at her, then shivered as a cold gust swept down from the mountain. "Mother Grint washed clothes on Mittwoch, and so do I — when I can."

"Do you wash because you bees a Lady?"

"And who said I am a Lady?"

---

[25] The name Wodenstag or 'Woden's Day' faded from German usage in the Middle Ages, replaced by Mittwoch.

"I see you bees a Lady. A Lady is like you. Is that why you wash your clothes and yourself so often?"

Ella thought on the question and answered honestly. "Washing is a habit and a custom. I like to be clean. The water is cold, but I feel good and alive after I wash. Fine clothes last longer when they are kept clean. Mother Grint taught me that dirt in clothing abrades the fibers."

"Our family weaves the best cloth in the mountains!" Ida declared proudly. "It'll last clean or dirty, and keeps peoples warm wet or dry! Silly to be washing clothes all the time. Can we wash my dress?"

"Yes! Go and fetch your blanket!" Ella laughed.

Ida sat wrapped in a blanket in the shelter. Her face shone pink and clean as she watched her dress and Ella's dry in the wind. Ella looked at her hands gently brushing the child's hair. *These are my mother's hands…*

Ida broke in on her thoughts. "Will we wash again next Mitt-woch? Will we wash our hair?"

"We will wash ourselves and our clothes next week– unless it is too cold. We will wash our hair when the flowers bloom!"

Dafid came into the fold and dragged the gate closed. "All the sheep are in now, but Blume was late again. She is limping." He pointed, "And look! Snow!" The girls looked up to see a gray pall of cloud where the mountain had been.

Ella woke in the night; the rising wind gusted bitterly cold. She pushed a heavy branch into the smoored fire, and pulled a fleece over Dafid and Ida. The storm blew until afternoon. At last, wind drove clouds from the sky, and a cold sun dazzled the white landscape.

Snows fell and melted. They grazed sheep in the shelter of the trees when the snow was deep, and on the benches when grass poked through. Often, as Ella read, or cooked, or washed, she saw little Ida watching, dark eyes intent. She mimicked Ella's manner of standing, of eating, of speaking, of walking and watching the sky. For her part, Ella learned much from the children who lived their lives barefoot in the mountains.

Dafid adored Ella. He brought her tiny presents of moss bound with grass stems, or colored stones from the creek. He stood abashed and delighted as she praised his gifts. He turned six on his gebutstag,[26] and slung stones with force and accuracy. The children throve on the simple, wholesome food Ella cooked for them. During the short daylight hours, they roamed with the flock. In the long twilight and darkness, they talked and laughed and sang the joy love put into their hearts. All slept in peace.

~

Blume grew thinner. "Etzel says you can't eat 'em when they're sick," Dafid said when Ella asked about the ewe. "When he comes next he will take her up to the ravine and skin her, and roll the carcass down."

The next morning the children lead the flocks to graze. Ella tied a cord around the docile ewe's neck, and led her toward the

---

[26] Gebutstag – 'birthday' *German.*

mountain. It took a long time, for the snow was deep in places, and Blume was weak and slow. Shadows were already lengthening when the bench finally broke into a deep, shadowy gorge. Beyond it the mountain rose steep and wild. Ella helped the old ewe, and skinned her. The sun dropped behind the ridge. Cold wind stiffened Ella's hands as she scraped and tugged at the skin.

At last Ella dragged the skin free, rolled it, and tied it with the cord. She stood, her back stiff and damp with sweat. Light faded. Clouds piled dark and ominous over the mountain above her. Ella shivered. She rolled the carcass over the edge, and it disappeared with a rattle of stones.

A howl split the twilight! Ella caught her breath. The wail came again – across the gorge – but close! Closer than Ella had ever heard before! With trembling hands she slung the bundled fleece over her shoulder. As she turned to retrace her steps to the fold, another howl came, and another – on her side of the gorge! Ella ran!

Down the hill, racing, falling, rising, plunging through snow, striking her feet on rocks, stumbling over hidden bushes. It was dark, the cloud-shrouded moon cast hardly a glimmer in the white, still world. She crashed into the woods, hoping she would not lose her way in the darkness. Ella heard no more howls. Lungs burning, she burst into a clearing. Ahead grew a single beech tree, its strong, bare arms reaching out against darkness and fear. She staggered to its bole, grasped the cord in her teeth, and jumped! Her hands clasped a bough and she scrambled into the safety of the tree's embrace. She turned and began pulling up the bundled fleece. Fangs flashed as a great gray shape sprang out of the darkness and sank its teeth into the sheepskin!

Ella's jaw struck the branch as the cord was yanked from her hands. The wolf fell to the snow, still clutching the skin. Instantly two more wolves tore into the fleece. Shreds of wool covered the ground in a moment. Transfixed, Ella watched as more wolves bounded into the clearing. One raced to the foot of the beech tree and looked up at her. Ella awoke from her trance and scrambled higher as the wolf rose on its hind legs and sniffed deeply. She almost fell in terror when it howled!

"Daddy! Daddy!" someone screamed. Ella gasped, took a deep, ragged breath; her mind cleared and she heard her own voice shouting, "Daddy charged the Turks!" Before her inner eye flashed eighteen-thousand sabers bright upraised, eighteen-thousand ribbons of steel against two-hundred-thousand Turks with musket, pike, and cannon.

"Praise the Lord my Rock!"
She sang out her father's Warrior Psalm,
"He trains my hands for war and battle!
God is my Ally! My Fortress,
My Citadel of Safety, my Rescuer,
My Buckler, my Mighty Savior!"
Her arms grew strong on the tree as she sang.

The night grew colder, wind tore clouds away from the moon, pouring light into the trampled meadow. No wolves. Ella strained her eyes, but saw no danger. She counted to a thousand, dropped from the tree, and ran!

"Ella! Ella!" Ida peeked out as Ella stumbled to the gate. "Ella, where have you been? We worried for you!"

Ella dragged the gate closed and sank to the ground, gasping. Dafid came near with a whimper, and Ella put her arms around the children. "I am here little ones, all is well. Build up the fire." They did, and Ella ate the porridge the children had kept warm. There was no reading that night. The children slept and Ella sat by the gate, trimming the end of her shepherd's staff into a sharp, three-sided point.

The sheep stood and shuffled restlessly. A frightened bleat. Ella stood and peered into the darkness. Shreds of cloud blew away from the moon. Cold light flowed over the snowy land.

A rustle. Ella turned to see a gray head and shoulders squeeze through the broken gate. Eyes glowed up at her, white teeth flashed. Ella screamed and thrust her spear into the neck of the wolf. It snarled and struggled, trapped in the wicker and bramble. Dafid shouted. Ella stabbed again. A cudgel flashed down, once, twice, the wolf was gone. Snarls and thrashing outside the gate. Ida stood close beside Ella, a cudgel in one hand and Ella's long knife in the other. Dafid shouted again and Ella glanced back to see a wolf tangled in the bramble atop the far wall of the fold. The boy's sling blurred in the moonlight; the wolf yelped and vanished. Then the gate sagged as a heavy body lunged against it. Ella stabbed through the wicker again and again. Ida was screaming, but Ella could not understand her. A stone whistled past and struck the wall. "Wedge the gate! Bring a branch!" Ella shouted, thrusting again with her spear. Ida was back, pushing against the gate with a branch. Ella dropped her spear, seized Ida's stick, bent to brace the wicker — then she was yanked to the ground and dragged into the broken gate. The wet wolf stank of starvation, of desperation! Thorns tore her hands; she groped for the knife in her belt. Ida's blade gleamed beside Ella's face, and the wolf let go. With desperate strength the child seized Ella's cloak and pulled her back from the gate. Ella leapt up and grabbed her spear.

Snow fell through the darkness. How long had it been snowing? How long had they fought? Ella did not know. It was quiet outside the fold. Ella shivered, she clung to the spear to keep her hands from trembling. The sheep huddled away from the body of a wolf that had fallen inside the fold, its skull fractured by Dafid's stone. Dark blood stained the trampled snow. Ella's knapsack and her long butcher knife lay by the gate.

Ella breathed deeply. "Praise the Lord my Rock who trains my hands for war...

"Dafid, build up the fire," she called, "Ida, bring long sticks from the woodpile!" The children obeyed. Ella wedged branches against the gate, blocking the hole, and holding it shut. She piled firewood against the gate and stood back.

The sheep had quieted. Night was silent. Snow still fell. She shivered in her damp clothes.

Dafid and Ida huddled close to the fire, cloaks steaming. Ella joined them. Dafid dragged a long, dry stick from the scattered pile of fuel and dropped one end in the coals. Ida lay down under the shelter, wrapped in her damp, woolen cloak. Ella spread a fleece over her. Then she sat by the fire with her legs drawn up and the spear in her hand. Dafid snuggled close. The snow stopped. The moon had gone. Starlight shone down. Fire slowly warmed her. Stars blurred.

Crash! The blow stunned her! Wolves!? No! Ella was choking, she struggled and rolled, trapped, and then free. Dafid was wailing beside her. Morning dim on the land. The shelter! The shelter roof had collapsed! Smoke rolled through the thatch!

Dafid was unhurt, eyes closed, mouth wide. Ida! Ella desperately dug into the smoking thatch, tearing the wet grass away. Sudden fire blazed up, she could not breathe! A foot! A corner of blanket! Ella seized Ida's leg and pulled! Trapped under the lintel! Ella grabbed the heavy pole and heaved; it came up with a burst of sparks and leaping flame. She gripped Ida's smoldering blanket and dragged her out of the fire, rolling the child over and over in the snow. She unwrapped the damp, steaming wool cloak. Gasping and crying, Ida came unhurt from the folds of heavy fabric. The fleece and the heavy woolen cloth had kept the fire from her.

Ida looked up from a face streaked with tears. "Oh Ella, your beautiful face! Your beautiful hair!" Sudden heat! Ella looked at her hands, her sleeves fell away in charred tatters. Her palms – the snow beneath them turned, green, then red, then black.

IX

The Shepherd's House

Spring sunshine poured through panes of glass onto the document before Ella. She heard a hoofclop in the street below, peered out, then dropped the parchment and hurried downstairs. Her hands hardly pained as she smoothed her short hair and pulled on her cap. She ran out in the street, turned through the yard, and into the stable.

Etzel looked up from the saddlepack and smiled at her. Ella didn't mind the twinge in her cheeks as she returned his smile. "How are the children?"

"The children miss you, but they are well. Grim and his dogs went back to his cottage today. He hasn't seen a wolf-track since winter, says they've gone back to the mountain. He found the heads of two wolves, says they likely died of their wounds and the pack ate them." He looked closely at her, "How are you feeling?"

Ella clasped her hands and looked down. "I am well, I feel well. But I am afraid that I will never spin and weave. Even with such good teachers, I don't seem to have the knack. I am only fit to cook. Your mother and sisters treat me very kindly. I haven't been so fussed over, since, well, ever. And your mother made me this." She pulled off her cap of blue lamb's-wool.

"It looks nice on you. It looks like your eyes, and maybe you should say that you are only fit to cook – and kill wolves!" Etzel's eyes smiled at her. "The flocks are heading up the mountain soon," He glanced in the direction of the peaks. "There will be the feast before we go, and dancing…"

Ella looked at the ground and fingered her cap. "I must go," she said, "Your people are so good to me, but the weather is fine for traveling, and I... should get on to Pierre's Chateau; my letter is more than six months old..."

Etzel looked at the saddlepack and nodded. "You are important to – to us. You know Mother and Father love you. You always have a home here with us..." He looked up and smiled. "Ida and Dafid are coming down today. Otto will stay with their sheep. I know the children will want to see you… Well, I am going to find father–"

"And I am going to the market for your mother."

"Then I will see you this afternoon. Bye for a while."

"Bye for a while," Ella answered, and hurried to the house for a basket.

A peddler, one Ella had never seen, had set up his wagon on the edge of the market. After making her purchases, she stopped to look at his eclectic treasures. The peddler watched attentively as she picked up one trinket after another. Some of the goods seem to have been damaged by fire. Three books sat together with covers burnt black and edges scorched, but their pages were solid. One book was a Latin commentary, another, also in Latin seemed to be a book of Roman thought. The third was a small Luther Bible printed with woodcut pictures. Ella felt the peddler's eyes on her. She passed on from the books, poked in a bowl of glass beads, fingered some fabric, and stopped at the end of the wagon.

She set down her knapsack, drew a quiet breath, and reached inside. There. Rag-wrapped. Hard, cool. Waiting for water.

She lifted it. Peeled the rags away. Spring sunshine glanced white and clean off the snowy peaks beyond the valley. Trees along the edge of the village lifted blossomed branches as the breeze shook them. Sunlight poured into the humble vessel, it glowed in Ella's hand. She looked at it for a moment, remembering the shivering cold of Patty's creek, the weary weight of the wooden spade, the labor of mixing and cutting, the hope with which she had set clay on the wheel, and the disappointment of failing again and again. The crushing realization that she was a burden to the people she loved. Kiln fire. The humbling wonder of finding that precious cup hidden among the foods Patty could scarce afford to share...

The peddler was still watching. Ella glanced up to see his eyes shrewdly flick from the cup to her face. She wiped away the emotion and lifted the cup. "Five kreuzer."

"It leaks," he retorted, but Ella had already won.

"Flawless. Five untrimmed silver coins." Ella repeated.

"How can I pa...iye...eal...ona....." the ringing in her ears drowned out his voice. She breathed deeply; she saw the man waving two fingers. She prepared to put the cup back into her knapsack, pretended to take a second glance at the goods, pretended to look at the cup again – but her vision blurred.

Ella looked up to the mountains, white and bright. *You are on a Journey*. She breathed the blossom-scented breeze. *There is future, hope, life...*

Her feet took her along the wagon, along the display of wares to the books. She saw clearly. And she heard the peddler whine, "...a poor man earn enough for bread?"

Ella tapped the charred Bible. "Three, and this, or I go!" He produced the coins and snatched the cup from her hands. It was still beautiful in his grasp. Light flowed out across the land, freed from the translucent cup. She set the coins between the pages of the Bible, put the book in her knapsack, and headed back toward the house with her basket.

Two small figures came walking down the road toward her. They broke into a run, and Ella set down her basket and ran to meet them. "Ida you are so clean and lovely! Dafid so tall, and what is this? A spear?" Ella laughed and the children laughed too.

"I have brought your Bible," Ida said, lifting the book from the sack at her side, "and your dictionary. I have read to Dafid every day!"

"And I can read too!" Dafid announced.

"Show me!" Ella invited. The three sat beside the road and Ida opened the Bible to the picture of the giant glowering at the shepherd boy.

"Here!" Dafid pointed, "and here! See? It is me! My name! Ida says so!"

"And it is you!" Ella laughed. "Sister Ida you have done well! I am proud of you both!

Today I went to the market to buy some greens for your mother, and I found this!" She took the Bible out of her knapsack.

"It has been burned…" Ida said in an awed voice. "Did King Jehoiakim do it?"

"I don't know how it was burned," Ella admitted, "but I don't think king Jehoiakim did it. Someday I will have it rebound. And this," she touched the Froschauer Bible, "is yours now. My family had it for a long time, and I want you, and your family Ida, to have it now, and the dictionary too. Read them to your children as my mother read them to me. I am very pleased with the way you have worked on your reading. Please keep reading, and Dafid you read too. David the King was a shepherd, and a mighty man of war, but he was also a learned man who could read the Law of God. It made him wise… mostly."

"I will!" Dafid vowed. The three took up the basket, and went on to the Shepherd Home.

~

Pink of early morning rippled under the cloud-barred sky, touching the snowy mountains with rose. The mule snorted, and followed the young man and the young woman out of the yard gate and through the quiet village. They walked in silence, wrapped in private thought. The land woke around them. The valley narrowed and lifted. Sunrise slid down the mountain wall and touched the trees above them. They stopped where the road split, Pierre's Mountain Chateau lay up the western road, the alpine pastures were above to the east.

"Farewell, Lady Davis." Etzel looked at her solemnly.

"Perhaps you will see your friend, Ella, again?" she asked.

Morning sun touched them, blazing her fringe of curls to copper and gold under the blue cap, lighting yellow depths in his brown eyes, and dark hair. "I would like that," he answered.

X

A Servant

"ierre! Pierre! Letter for Pierre!" The aging host hurried from his larder to see a young woman at his kitchen half-door. Blue eyes smiled merrily in a face deeply scarred. Bright hair peeked from under her woven cap. She held a letter.

"Yes, yes dear, I am he, and the blessing of St. Gabriel be upon you. There is milk in a jug in the cistern,[27] be refreshed." He

---

[27] Cistern: An enclosed basin to catch and hold water, sometimes jars or pots were placed into the cistern to keep cool.

hobbled close and took the letter. The young woman pulled up the jar of milk and drank gratefully.

Pierre scanned the letter and looked again at the girl who sat by the cistern with clasped hands, gazing out over the mountain valley. "You are Ella?" He asked. She looked up, solemn now, and nodded. Pierre rubbed his chin and said aloud to himself, "The house has guests due this very night, they will want entertaining, and it is not easy for an old man to scamper up and down stairs… You can wash linens and air beds and entertain guests?" he wondered.

"Monsieur, I will do the work," Ella allowed, "but I will not have the guests, nor anyone else take any liberty with me." Her eyes, so merry before, were glacier-cold now.

"No no! Mademoiselle, have no worry here!" Pierre stammered, "Jacques, he said you were virtuous as the maid Joan herself – perhaps you are fierce as she also! No worry here! My house is renowned for the hunting and the feasting, oui and the fishing too! But I would never have that sort here! No! I would be ashamed, and the Virgin herself would be ashamed of me too! Mademoiselle Ella, this is a safe place for you! I read in the letter that it was no fault of yours, no fault to you that you left the palace kitchen. I think you will be glad here, and I will be too!"

So it was that Lady Ella Davis made her swiftest conquest.

Pierre's alpine valley lay all in shadow as afternoon lights slid up the eastern slopes to flash brilliant white and gold and blue on the peaks. Hooves clattered below. Ella straightened the last bed, fluffed the feather pillows, and looked from the dormer window. Horses stamped in the yard. Men swung down as the hostler came to greet them. A gray horse, a tall man in a dusty tabard, head thrown back, laughing, golden-haired, his arm around the shoulders of a younger man… Ella's breath caught in her throat. Gilbert! And the prince!

She must not be caught in the bedrooms! *To the board! They will go first to the board!* Ella rushed downstairs and took refuge in the kitchen. She flitted from one task to the next, trying to ignore the voices and laughter from the dining hall.

Evening, and Pierre poked his head into the kitchen. "Mademoiselle, I must step out for a few moments. The gentlemen are still eating. When you clear the board, notice if the wine is low, and bring more up from the cellar – and do not wipe the bottles!" He was gone, Ella was left nodding woodenly.

It was time to serve brioche.[28] Ella lifted the basket, took a deep breath, and passed into the feast. Six men sat at table, they reached for the basket as she set it down; two men glanced at her curiously, the prince and Gilbert did not look up. Ella released

---

[28] Brioche is a light yeast bread with a crisp and flaky brown crust. Sometimes sweet, often garnished and served as a dessert.

the breath she had held. Yes, the wine was low. Quickly she gathered empty dishes onto a tray and hurried from the room. She took the key, hurried down cellar, and returned with four bottles. Pierre was not back. As she stepped into the dining hall, her eyes met Gilbert's. His bleary expression did not change. His gaze passed from her face down to the bottles. He grinned and raised a hand. She carried the wine to him.

"I'll open these myself," he said without looking up, and reached for the corkscrew.

Ella gathered a tray of used crockery and went to the kitchen with Mother Grint's words echoing in her memory, "He never saw you…"

~

The prince and his companions spent a week at the Chateau, hunting and riding. Then one evening, strange men came on tired horses. They sat long, closeted with the prince. Pierre sent Ella to her chamber. "Lock the door *ma fille*, I will wait on these men and hear nothing they say. Do not come out until after light tomorrow." In the morning, when Ella woke and carried water from the spring, the strangers were already gone. That day the prince and his people departed.

"Go walking today," Pierre urged her. "Pack a little snack and walk on the mountain. We have no guests in the house, and violets are blooming on the mountain."

But it was down the valley that her feet took her. She paused in the shady gap at the valley's foot, and sat on a stone, listening to the gurgle of water from a little spring on the hillside. Long ago someone had chiseled a channel in the stone. Water flowed down the rock to pool in a basin for the relief of travelers. The shrine there had been toppled in some fit of reforming zeal. Like many other things once honored, it now lay mossy, neglected, forgotten. Ella looked down into the still water. A young woman gazed up at her. A thin face, and tired, bright hair pulled back, cheeks scarred, blue eyes thoughtful... Gilbert had never looked at her again. He had not been rude – just indifferent. Who is the woman in the pool? *Ella Davis… What does it mean to be Ella Davis… ?* She sighed.

Someone stood near her on the road. Ella jumped to her feet. "Etzel!"

He smiled. "May I say 'Ella'?"

She laughed, "Yes! What brings you here?"

"I could ask that of you! Our shepherds have supplies for a fortnight, the children are well, father gave me leave, and I came to see you!" His voice grew suddenly hollow as he asked, "Are you waiting for someone?"

"Will you climb with me?" she asked. "Will you come on the mountain and see the violets?"

And he did.

~

In the deep cold after Yule, Etzel came again. Ella heard the clomp of iron shoes outside, and Pierre welcoming someone. She hurried to the common room to find Etzel and Pierre by the warm hearth. Both men turned toward her as she came in. Pierre's wide palm patted Etzel's back so that he staggered. The old man's eyes were bright and moist as he looked away. "You two had better be hurrying on. The Chateau can last without her until twelfth-night." Ella fled, and was back in a moment, dressed in all her clothes with her knapsack on her back. Etzel took her by the hand and they went out into the dim light of a cloudy winter noon. It was too cold for talk. Etzel pulled a blanket off the mule, helped Ella up on his back, and wrapped the blanket around her. He turned and hurried down the road with the mule following after.

Hearthlight flowed across the snow as the door swung open. The family tumbled out to greet them, to lift Ella down, to brush the snow from her cloak. Embraces, and pats, and a happy babble of welcome. Mr. Shepherd took the mule, and Mrs. Shepherd led the young people into the house by the fire. The sisters crowded close, and Ida was with them. "Dafid is with Grim and the sheep," she said. "He would not come – he is hoping that the wolves will come again and he will get a wolfskin!"

Light and laughter, stories of old times, feasting and song. Ida sat by the tallow candle and read to the family how 'mountains had been made low, and the valleys raised up,' and how the Good Shepherd had come to be the Savior of the World, and how the angels had brought the news first to shepherds! It was the merriest Yule that Ella had ever known.

A milky river of stars flowed across the sky, from the rumpled white western peaks, to the more rounded mountains of the east. The night was windless and bitter cold. Their steps raised tiny, glittering puffs of snow. Far-off, a tree cracked in the starlight. Ella's feet were cold. Breath tingled and drifted for a moment before her face as she adjusted her muffler. Etzel stood beside her, silent, looking away to the mountain wall. Far off, a wolf howled. Ella shivered and Etzel asked, "Cold?"

"I am well!" and she meant it. Behind them was a house warm with family and feasting, bright with love. Before them a vast, clean world of stars and hope.

"Lady Davis… I do not know whom to ask…" Etzel began.

"Ask Ella," her response was quiet, gentle, decided.

His gloved hand touched her arm. He turned toward her, a glimmer of starlight in his dark eyes. "Ella, will you marry me?"

"I will."

XI

Home

Four fine horses stood in the yard beside the Shepherd house. Spring wind carried the scent of all things growing, and the song of birds, as well as the whistling of the shepherds and the bleating of their sheep as the flocks began their migration[29] up the mountain toward summer pasture. "Mary," Ella called, "please find your brother, and both of you

---

[29] Transhumance migration of livestock between lower and higher altitudes is a traditional practice in many cultures.

come to the kitchen. Oma has a treat for you!"

A dark-haired, blue-eyed girl of six danced past her mother into the yard, and returned dragging a distressed two-year-old boy. "Isht! Isht!" he cried, pointing at the horses. He quieted when Grandmother Shepherd brought out a tray of rolls.

Ida came in, tall and lovely, her skin dark from the sun, her long, brown hair pulled back. She greeted Ella with a smile. Ella laughed, "Happy birthday! Fifteen and blooming like a mountain-flower!"

Ida blushed and curtseyed. "Father spent all morning talking with that merchant, but I just saw him depart. Let's go and see what happened!"

"I had better stay in sight of the cookie-eaters," Ella said, "I will wait for your report."

Upstairs, a strange man in fine clothes sat writing at the table. Mr. Shepherd stood smiling out the open window. He turned when he heard Ida's step and held out his arms. "Birthday Flower!" he laughed, "It is a great day for the Shepherd Family! I have concluded an agreement with the merchant who just left – his clerk is writing out the contract for us now. He will buy a great quantity of worsted – for uniforms I think – and we shall fill the contract! It is to be delivered to Genoa[30] before the autumn storms." He leaned close and whispered to his daughter. Her eyes widened. Her father nodded. "And we shall pay back all the money I borrowed to buy the flocks! And you and Dafid shall come down from the mountain and sleep in beds! If next year the contract is renewed, we will buy land!"

"Oh Daddy!" Ida exclaimed, "This is wonderful! Please show me the contract!" Mr. Shepherd gestured to the table and turned back to the window with a smile.

As Ida walked to the table, the clerk looked up angrily and made to cover his writing. "May I have it?" Ida asked.

---

[30] Genoa is important commercial city on the northwest side of the Italian peninsula between the Mediterranean Sea, and Central Europe. It was a banking center, as well as a point of departure for European goods.

But he growled, "Go away child! Business is for men!" The clerk had the look of a shrewd man who knew how to sell information, a man who might have business partners his merchant employer knew nothing of.

"Give me the paper!" Ida demanded, "Papa, this man –"

Mr. Shepherd turned from his reverie, "Hand her the agreement at once!" The clerk darted his eyes to the side and obeyed.

Ida scanned the paper, her lips moving as she read, she read it again and looked at her father. "The price written here is the one you told me, and the amount of wool, but it says in this paper that you are responsible to ship it over the water! Papa we have no boats! And the corsairs – You will be robbed, enslaved!"

Mr. Shepherd looked angrily at the clerk. "Your master and I agreed that I would deliver the wool to his warehouse in Genoa! That is already a very long road from here. What is this about shipping across the water?"

The clerk licked his lips, "Perhaps the child misread, it is script and a girl might –"

"No!" Ida's voice was hard. She handed the paper to her father.

He did not pretend to read it. "Write the contract again – write it as your master and I agreed!" He fixed the clerk with a hard stare. "Or shall I call your master back so we can all discuss this?"

The clerk shook his head. "It is a misunderstanding easily put right." He drew another sheet from his folio, cleaned, dipped, and blotted his pen, and began to write. Ida stood beside him, reading each word he wrote. The clerk completed the document, sanded it, and handed it to Ida. His face had no expression.

Ida read the paper aloud to her father, enunciating each word. Mr. Shepherd listened, nodding. At last, he took the paper and made his mark at the bottom. The clerk dripped wax onto the document and pressed it with his master's seal. He folded his writing kit, bowed, and departed.

~

Laughter filled the manor house garden where Mary played with the little children. Davis was out with his father, walking the lands they had bought. He and Etzel were inspecting the neglected fields, talking about how to rebuild the soil, which trees to cut, and how many years the land should be grazed and manured before it was productive for crops again.

A rattle of leaves blew past Ella into the kitchen as she stepped through the open door. The table was gone, and the chairs. The room was bare, the floor strewn with dry leaves. Black embers lay cold on the hearth. It smelled deserted. The door to the dining hall dragged as Ella pushed it open. She glanced out the kitchen door to where the children played, and then passed through the dining hall into the Long Gallery.

Dim.

Echoing.

Empty.

Windows gray with dust and cobwebs. There were no furnishings, no hangings of weapons, no portraits. Against one wall hung a heavy drapery. Ella's heart fluttered. She stood before the tapestry.

Was it a unicorn? Faded and moldering, it was hard to tell, but looking at it with the memory of a child, she imagined a circle of golden trees, and in the center, a blur of white... As she had seen her mother do so often, Ella rippled the edge of the tapestry and stepped behind it. In the darkness her hand slid over stone, then wood, and touched iron. She drew the key from around her neck and slid it into the lock. It turned. Silently, the door swung inward.

Diffused light trickled from above, bathing an empty plinth. Dust motes danced, like words in the books that filled dark shelves with memory and mystery. She almost heard her mother's voice in the quiet...

Epilogue

Gilbert the butler smiled like a man glad to have a job. His florid face beamed welcome at the guests as they entered the hall. They were humble guests, merchants, artisans, a protestant minister, land-holding farmers, and a few industrious nobles with mercantile connections to the host and his wife. The prince would not grace this celebration with his presence – not that he was too proud, but his feet hurt, and he retired early. The prince made no secret that he was glad of the revenue such celebrations brought. It was expensive to maintain a palace.

Sweet music swelled to fill the ballroom, couples swayed across the floor. The great room hummed with gentle laughter and conversation. Happy children skipped and scampered among the dancers. Etzel and Ella swirled in the center of it all, surrounded by trusted friends, by children and grandchildren, by memories of thirty five years lived together in love, and faith, and honor.

Like a story.

fin

Printed in the USA
CPSIA information can be obtained
at www.ICGtesting.com
LVHW061124170823
755276LV00003B/401